THE CURSED ARROW

Elli Buchanan

The Cursed Arrow
(A Paranormal Romance)

1

By

Elli Buchanan

THE CURSED ARROW
Short Story
(A Paranormal Romance)

Elli Buchanan
PUBLISHED BY:

Copyright © 2016
www.booksbyellibuchanan.com

The Cursed Arrow

Chapter 1

A perfectly curated museum should give a visitor the same feeling of awe and reverence as entering a holy place. It is where history meets the present, and people can discover new and revealing ways to cope with the cares and worries they have in common with their ancestors.

That's how Antonia Selman had always thought a museum should be. It was the way she viewed it as a young girl, and the feeling only grew with time and understanding. Museums were her gateway into the wider world, and she felt comfort in their history filled rooms.

But she also realized, as she walked slowly through the softly lit corridors of the old, refurbished mansion, that the grandness of a museum out of opening hours, could also be a little intimidating and eerie.

She gripped her black bag tightly to her side and tried to slow her pace so the clicking of her heels echoed less in the emptiness.

Calm down. I belong here now, she thought. There was a little white ID tag with her picture, clipped to her black cardigan to prove it. It showed her face with a serious expression befitting her new role as assistant curator with her thick dark hair pulled back in a tight twist, as it was today. *There's no reason for me to feel anxious.*

But it was her first day on the job and the fact that she had lost her way trying to find the employee entrance, didn't do much to settle her nerves.

She heard sounds. Someone was talking. At that moment a uniformed museum guard appeared around the corner, his head down as he released the button on the walkie-talkie at his shoulder. His conversation had cloaked the sound of Antonia's heels, so he had no warning of her presence, which was obvious by the startled look on his face. He stared at her with wide eyes before reason took over and he knew she was not a piece of artwork come to life.

'Ma'am, the museum won't be open for another two hours.'

'I'm new here,' Antonia said as she showed him her badge. 'I'm trying to find the employee entrance,' she continued to explain. 'But you're first real person I've come across since I came in.'

'Did you come in through the back?'

She shook her head.

The young man nodded, as if he'd been able to figure out everything just by asking her that one question. 'It's not a big deal. Usually employees park around the back. Someone should have told you. Follow me, I'll show you where to go.'

He led her to the end of the hallway where an unmarked door blended into the wall. He held his ID card to a thin black electronic strip and the door clicked open with a beep.

Antonia laughed in surprise. 'A hidden door.'

The guard grinned mischievously. 'Yeah, the whole place is one giant Scooby-Doo set.'

Antonia smiled at him. 'Thank you...?'

'Miles, Miles Dunne,' he said, offering her a brief handshake.

'Antonia Selman,' she replied as the door began to beep violently.

He nudged her. 'It's a security warning. You'd better go.'

'Of course.' She jumped through the opening and was barely able to wave goodbye to Miles before he closed the door, and the alarm was silenced.

The hallway in front of her was cold and austere, vastly different from the rich colors and gentle lighting in the museum. She ignored the contrast and purposefully walked towards the white door at the far end.

Antonia had expected the offices to be similar to the libraries at her university, quiet and studious. Instead, everything was in chaos. No one noticed her arrival. The room held a sea of desks, computers and the everyday things of any busy office. Personal knick-knacks and photos added a personal touch to the expected file trays, stacks of paper and copious numbers of used coffee cups.

Some workers moved between the desks, delivering papers to those who were furiously typing on keyboards, others were stacking and documenting items on a long table that ran the length of the room.

'What year was Piece 57 from?'

'Who was the old guy who gave us Piece 378? The one who smelled like gin?'

'Who the hell labeled Piece 690 as an 'ancient back scratcher'? Have you no pride in your work?'

'Hey, there is some solid evidence to support that claim.' A low rumble of laughter moved across the room.

'Okay, people,' a woman yelled from the doorway of an attached office. She looked as tightly wound as the French twist in her blonde hair. 'We have a client coming in soon, so while I appreciate that you are all working hard, can we try not to look like disorganized rabble?'

She glanced at the entrance and spotted Antonia. 'Ms. Selman?' she called, and Antonia nodded. The woman quickly made her way toward her before thrusting out her hand and gripping Antonia's in a firm handshake. 'Pamela Morgan. I'm glad you're here. As you can see it's bedlam today.'

'I'm sorry I'm late; I got a bit turned aroun....'

'Don't worry about that,' the woman snapped. Her grip on Antonia's arm was firm enough to be uncomfortable as she pulled her towards the other side of the room. 'One of our guys just called in sick, burst appendix or something. Can you work the HIDT system?'

'The online information drive? Of course, I used it at my last internship.'

The stress melted from the woman like butter in a microwave. 'Thank God. I'll get you set up.'

'But what about my other work?'

'Ms Morgan,' one of the workers interrupted. 'Can you tell if this pot is Osage or Makah?' He swiveled the computer around to face them both.

Antonia recognized it immediately. 'It's Osage.'

They looked at her skeptically.

'It's the color of the clay that gives it away,' Antonia explained. 'The Osage lived in lands with lots of red clay. The Makah didn't.'

Pamela raised a brow, silently questioning why he hadn't thought of that himself. She turned to Antonia. 'Ms Selman, walk with me.'

Antonia obeyed without question. She followed the tall blond past the desks and up a flight of simple wooden stairs to another floor of offices, just as chaotic as the first. 'Unfortunately, you've joined us at a busy time, Ms Selman. We have a charity gala in eight days, and everyone is scrambling to get things together. I've been on the phone with four different caterers all morning long. Your job...' she paused. 'What was your job again?'

'Assistant curator of the Mesoamerican culture exhibit.'

'That's right. You're the mythology girl.'

Antonia's ears burned. 'I think of it as a part of ancient cultural-anthropology and...'

Pamela cut in. 'Yes, yes. Now, it will be up to you to get the pieces for your exhibit in order so that we can impress the patrons. You can start that tomorrow, but for today I want you working on the HIDT system and getting that finished. Your desk is here.' She stopped next to an empty chair.

Antonia stared blankly at it for a moment, trying to mentally recover from the chaos of the last ten minutes. 'Ms Morgan, if you don't mind me asking,' she said. 'I thought I was assisting Ms Tovo with the Mesoamerican exhibit.'

'That's right.'

'So why isn't she here explaining all of this to me?'

Pamela blinked, then threw back her head and laughed. 'Oh honey. Didn't you know? Ms Tovo is the director of the museum. She's got a lot more on her plate than that.'

Chapter 2

When she arrived home, Antonia threw her apartment keys into the little blue souvenir plate with exhausted accuracy.

'Hello?' she called.

A cheerful voice answered from the living room. 'Hey, I'm in here. How was work?' The voice belonged to a young woman Antonia's age. She was sitting on the couch in the same sweatpants and t-shirt she had on when Antonia left the house that morning.

'Did you change at all?' Antonia asked.

The young woman shrugged. 'I've been busy. I had like a million things to do online today. I haven't even showered yet, see?' She pulled at a piece of her bobbed blonde hair. 'Disgusting.'

Antonia grinned. 'How would the Birdie groupies react if they knew Katie Bird wasn't as glamorous as her avatar?'

Katie waved it off. 'They'll forgive me. Now tell me about your first day at work.'

In lieu of actually answering, Antonia crossed the room and threw herself into the big, overstuffed arm-chair with a grunt.

'That sounds promising.'

'It's insane.'

'Oh no, did someone pilfer the Mona Lisa again?'

'No. But I'm basically in charge of my whole gallery.'

Katie squinted and cocked her head to one side, a habit that made her look like a suspicious cocker-spaniel. 'I'm sorry, but how is that a bad thing?'

'It's so much work.'

'But I thought you liked working alone.'

'I do,' Antonia answered. 'But this is a big deal. My boss, the one I was supposed to be assisting, is the director of the whole museum.'

Katie looked even more confused. 'Wait, so she's the director of the museum and the curator of your gallery?'

Antonia nodded solemnly.

'Why the hell would she do that?'

Antonia shrugged. 'I don't know. I think the gallery is kind of her baby, and she didn't want to give it up.'

'So, she's not going to manage you, but still micro-manage you at the same time. Sounds like the worst scenario possible.'

Antonia shook her head. 'I don't know. I didn't even get to meet her today. There's a charity gala in a week, and everyone's running around like mad trying to get that straightened out.'

Katie considered the situation. 'I'm sure you'll be fine. You're made for this kind of craziness.'

'No, I'm not.'

'Oh yes you are,' Katie replied sternly. 'You're the one who wrote the best essays five hours before they were due.'

'How would you know? You're not in my field.'

'But I am a paid blogger,' Katie replied. 'I know a good paper when I see one.'

Antonia rolled her eyes but laughed. 'We'll see how this goes.'

'Of course, we will. In the meantime, we need to tackle the most important questions like-'

'Katie, no.'

'Come on,' her roommate whined. 'You can't tell me there isn't a single attractive guy working there?'

Antonia sighed. 'I don't know. I was too busy to pay attention.'

'Well pay attention next time,' Katie said. 'You're my blog's pet project. If I can guide you into a good relationship, then we'll know my advice is worth something.'

Katie shook her head. Getting a date for Antonia was one of Katie's favorite past-times. She'd insisted her friend get out more during university, but Antonia had insisted right back that her master's degree was more important. 'I can date when I'm done with this,' she'd say after turning down a night-out for a study all-nighter.

But the truth was that Antonia just wasn't interested in most of the guys she met. Sure, they were fun and usually nice looking, but none of them seemed to engage her. She wanted someone who liked her quirks and her obsessions with history. As much as Katie said otherwise, Antonia doubted she would meet such a man in a dark bar.

Katie shook her head. 'Right, well I've been home all day, and I'm going to go crazy if I don't leave this house now.'

Antonia whined, 'Can't we just stay in?'

'Toni. I have been here all day. I haven't even put a bra on.'

'I thought that was a sign of victory.'

Her roommate threw a pillow at her. 'Come on, get yourself up.'

'Katie, I really don't want to go out tonight. Can't we compromise?'

'Who said anything about going out?' Katie asked incredulously. 'I just want to go to the supermarket to get some ice cream. We're watching movies tonight.'

That idea was much more appealing to Antonia, so she hoisted herself out of the armchair and into her room to peel off her heels and stockings.

'What movie you want to watch?' Katie called from her own room across the hall.

'Anything but horror, thank you.'

Her roommate leaned in her doorway, working a glob of dry shampoo through her hair. 'What is it with you and horror films anyway?'

'What do you mean?'

'Well, your career is studying historical horror stories, and....'

'Ancient spirituality and local legends are not horror stories,' Antonia interrupted.

'And' continued her friend, 'You are terrified of horror movies. I don't get it.'

Antonia grabbed a clean pair of shorts from her closet. 'I don't know. Horror movies just don't interest me.' This was a true statement of course, but what Antonia didn't say was her family's history of dabbling in dark magic and the spirit realms, left her a little reluctant to watch it on TV as well. Her grandmother had stepped away from the family heritage when she married, but she always made it very clear to Antonia that the spiritual realm was not one to be messed with.

'No horror movies,' Grandmama would always say to little Antonia as she sat on her lap and listened to the stories of the Old Times. 'I don't want to invite any of that nonsense into my home. You know how long it takes to exorcise a spirit? Even a benign one can take weeks. I once had a summer spirit living in my refrigerator for three months.'

Antonia let loose her heavy black hair and straightened her white T-shirt. It looked good against her dusky skin and was one-hundred-percent more comfortable than the suit she'd worn to work.

'Can't we just watch Bridesmaids again?'

Katie shrugged. 'We'll talk about it on the way. Come on, I want to get out of this place.'

Chapter 3

The charity gala was being held soon and work had been a non-stop flurry of panic since Antonia's first day.

Pamela Morgan had set her to work entering information into the online database. She knew the patrons would be asking detailed questions about the exhibit items on the night, and she needed something to show them for their generous donations.

'For a bunch of rich old people, they are obsessed with us having the latest technology,' Ms. Morgan had muttered under her breath.

On top of this Antonia had to complete the preparations for the Mesoamerican exhibit. She still hadn't met Ms. Tovo, but every day there was a new list of tasks waiting for her in her inbox. Her absentee boss was nothing if not organized.

With only three days until the gala, Antonia was about two tasks into the day's work when Pamela came to her desk.

'Did you manage to finish the work on the database?'

Antonia nodded. 'I've finished the bulk of it today, now I'm trying to get some of these things –'

'I really appreciate everything you're doing,' Pamela cut her off. 'But I would feel so much better if you were able to complete these data reports.'

Antonia bit her tongue. 'Of course. Do you know when Ms. Tovo will be coming in?'

At that moment the double doors to the office opened and a glamorous couple entered, laughing and chatting together. Antonia guessed the woman to be in her late thirties.

I wonder if this is the director, at last? she thought absently, as her gaze moved to the strikingly handsome man at the blond woman's side. He was tall and dark with angular features. Tanned skin stretched over a strong jaw and high cheek bones. His smile was dazzling, and Antonia's stomach did a little flip. She was silently surprised at her reaction. When was the last time *that* had happened? She couldn't remember. She mentally shook herself. *Don't be ridiculous Antonia. Look at them. They're obviously a couple.*

The woman's dress was of fine silk and flowed around her slim body like water. Her immaculately coffered hair was swept up in a sophisticated chignon and her face was porcelain perfect. *She's beautiful,* Antonia had to grudgingly admit. Her gaze drifted to the man and her stomach again gave another involuntary flip-flop. If a man could be called beautiful, then he was beautiful too. Everything about him, from his grey suit to the way he moved, spoke of confidence, power and wealth.

'I understand your misgivings, Hunter,' the woman said with a coy smile. 'But our historians have already taken a look at the arrowhead, and we all agree that–'

'And I understand what you're saying, Sonia,' the man said. 'But with priceless artifacts such as this, especially one that is so close to my heart, you'll understand if I'm reluctant to put it on display.'

Ah, thought Antonia. They're not a couple. An unexpected feeling of relief washed over her as she listened quietly to their conversation.

'Our security systems are state of the art,' Sonia Tovo answered encouragingly. 'The arrow that killed the Sabre-man's wife would be the prize of the gala.'

'But it's only a story, Sonia,' he replied with a smile.

'Yet you treasure it as your most valuable piece.'

The man stayed firm. 'Nevertheless, I've made my decision.'

Sonia's smile became strained. 'Of course, Hunter,' she said with disappointment. 'I just know how much it would impress the gala guests, especially as a crowning piece to the rest of your excellent donations.'

But the man was no longer listening. His gaze swept the room, intense and scrutinizing. His dark eyes narrowed, and his body tensed as his search stopped at Antonia.

The director looked to the reason for her guest's distraction. 'Oh, you must be my new assistant,' she said, moving straight towards Antonia with her own huntress-like intensity. 'Ms. Selman, isn't it?'

Antonio tore herself away from Hunter's piercing gaze and turned to face her boss. 'It's so nice to finally meet you, Ms. Tovo.'

'Please call me Sonia.' She shook her hand firmly. 'I was just showing Mr. Hunter our gallery. You have done an excellent job of following my directions.'

Hunter approached them, more relaxed now. 'Emmanuel Hunter.' He reached out his hand to introduce himself.

The moment Antonia touched him, she was overwhelmed by a sense of nostalgia. She felt every part of his rough palms against her soft hands, and she was hardly able to breathe. The feelings washed over her. They felt like the warmth of remembrance and a sense of home; but also, a fissure of excitement and longing blended together to stimulate her senses in a brief explosion of sensation.

Hunter yanked back his hand like he'd been burned, and coughed to cover his own surprise. 'Ms. Selman, your exhibit is coming along nicely. Ms. Tovo has been an excellent guide for you.'

Feeling confused at the feelings that merely touching his hand had brought, she blinked and stammered a reply, 'A-absolutely. Ms Tovo is an excellent administrator.'

The older woman was looking at her client and her new employee suspiciously; however, the comments seem to soothe her.

'That's very sweet of you to say, Ms. Selman,' Sonia answered, still frowning slightly at the undercurrent she noticed between the two. 'Have you two met before?'

Antonia quickly shook her head and Hunter's voice was gravelly. 'No,' he answered as he turned his back on Antonia. 'She's doing well then?' Hunter asked Sonia as he touched her elbow and led them both away from her desk.

Antonia's face colored in embarrassment. *How rude,* she fumed as she watched them walk away, discussing her as though she wasn't in the room.

'Yes, we're quite pleased with her,' Sonia responded. 'But now, about the Aztec headdress that you mentioned. I'm interested in where you found it.'

Sonia Tovo guided Hunter away from the offices, leaving Antonia sitting numbly at her desk as Pamela Morgan entered the room.

'Are you alright?' the other woman asked.

Antonia nodded. 'I'm fine,' she replied. She returned to her work quietly and tried to ignore the way her hands were shaking.

Chapter 4

A few hours of intense work and discussions with Pam Morgan did nothing to calm Antonia's nerves, but at the very least they put her experience into a much better light. She still remembered Hunter's strange behavior towards her, and the more she thought about it, the more it occurred to her that she'd seen that expression before. It was the universal look of a historian who has just discovered something entirely out of place, like finding a 500-year-old artifact in a 2000-year-old archeological dig.

The powerful feeling of reminiscence that had come over her when she took his hand, still lingered. Antonia might have chalked it up to attraction, the kind you hear about in love stories that start with the words 'When I met her, I just knew...'. But she was too sensible for that. She knew that 'love-at-first sight' stories weren't real. Besides, who said that what she'd felt was love? It was powerful for sure, but love? Towards a man she'd literally just been introduced to? Ridiculous.

Still, she found herself thinking about Hunter throughout the day. Images of his broad shoulders would float through her head while she classified paintings. The feeling of his warm hand sent tingles down her spine while she typed up her reports. The way he carried himself, so self-assured and even a little arrogant, crossed her mind more than once.

It was annoying. She had work to do. But the more she tried to put him out of her mind, the more he invaded her thoughts.

And that evening, Katie did absolutely nothing to help the situation.

'How was work?' she asked politely when Antonia entered the kitchen to find an after-work snack.

'Fine,' Antonia answered, but then Hunter popped into her mind again. The thought of his rough hand against her soft palm washed over her. She tried to hide her blush by diving into the refrigerator.

But it was too late. Katie was grinning at her like a cat with a bowl of cream.

'Work was fine?' Katie asked.

'It was fine.'

Her roommate arched her eyebrows. 'Was it fine, or was it *fine*?'

Antonia blushed again. 'Shut up.'

Katie took a deep, excited breath. 'You met someone. What happened? Is he cute? Is it that security guard guy?'

Antonia saw no escape. She knew that Katie would hound her relentlessly until she had the details. 'No, it's not Miles. I just met a patron of the museum.'

'So, this patron's into history? That's a good start,' Katie replied cheerfully. 'Is he cute?'

Antonia brushed the hair back from her face and looked away. 'He's not bad.'

'Oh, this is just the *best* day,' Katie squealed. 'What else do you know about him?'

'Nothing,' Antonia answered emphatically. Yet even as she said it, she felt in her gut that wasn't true. 'I don't know. I feel like I've met him before.'

'Huh? At university maybe?'

Antonia shook her head. It was doubtful. It's not like she made a point to rub elbows with the rich and glamorous during her uni days. In fact, probably the most glamorous thing she'd had contact with for the last six years were the plush reading rooms of the university library.

'Well, I'm sure you'll figure it out,' Katie said off-handedly. 'When are you going to see him again?'

Antonia cocked her head to the side. The thought of seeing Hunter again hadn't crossed her mind. He was a wealthy and successful man of the world, and she was... busy. 'I probably won't,' she said.

Katie was having none of that. 'Absolutely unacceptable. This is the first guy I've seen you blush over in three years. You are not letting this one get away from you.'

'What am I supposed to do?' Antonia asked. 'Find his address in the company registry and show up on his doorstep?'

For a moment her roommate seemed to be considering the thought, but eventually she dismissed it. 'No, we can't really come up with an excuse for that right now,' she said. 'But if he's going to be at this charity gala thing...'

'Katie, he's a patron. I can't just...'

'Sure, you can.' Katie waved away any excuses that Antonia might throw at her. 'Impress him with your brain like you always do... and wear red.'

ooooo

At 3am Antonia shot up from her pillow, shaking violently and afraid of what she might see in the shadows. It took her a few moments to realize she had not really escaped from a dark creature with long teeth and thousands of hands that grabbed at her ankles while she ran.

She reached to turn on the bedside lamp, jumping when the cord brushed her skin. There was nothing there, of course. The creature wasn't real, and although she felt she'd run for miles, she'd only been dreaming.

Antonia suddenly had an intense longing for her grandmother, who used to wrap her up in her arms when she had a nightmare as a little girl. But against all reason, she also wanted to go back into the dream. She'd left someone behind there, a man who loved her. She wanted to find him and make sure he was safe, that the monster with the many arms hadn't hurt him.

'It was just a dream,' Antonia whispered. But she couldn't forget the grip of the monster as it grabbed at her ankles. She sat up and pulled her knees to her chest, eventually falling asleep with the light on.

Chapter 5

For once Sonia Tovo was in her office, sitting at her desk and going over paperwork. Antonia was relieved at first, but as the day went on, she felt more and more nervous. Sonia hadn't once talked to her about any of the projects she'd been working on. In fact, it seemed as though her boss didn't know she was there at all.

It must mean I'm doing a good job, Antonia told herself during her coffee break. *If she's not on to me about something, then I guess nothing's wrong.*

Antonia couldn't have been more mistaken.

'Antonia, will you come into my office for a moment?'

Antonia pushed back her chair, bumping her knee in her haste. She straightened her skirt, took a deep breath and walked into the office. 'Yes, Ms. Tovo?'

'I told you, call me Sonia. Please sit down.' Her glasses were perched on her nose, making her seem much older than she'd appeared yesterday. But still, with her crisp white shirt and grey pearls, she was as elegant as ever. 'I want to thank you for all your hard work.'

'Oh, it's no...'

Ms. Tovo held up a single finger. Antonia stopped talking.

'I want to thank you,' she continued. 'But some of this is not quite up to snuff. I'll need you to reorganize the clay relics according to date, but I also need you to make the display look attractive, cohesive.' She searched her desk until she found a stack of papers marked over with red that she handed to Antonia. 'Also, there's been a problem with Items 64-103 on the online database which need to be corrected immediately. I'll need both of these tasks completed before you leave.'

Antonia held her hand out for the papers. Nothing Sonia had said was all that bad, but Antonia still had the distinct impression she was being scolded for something. 'I'll get right on it.'

'Excellent. You may go.'

Antonia closed the door to the office and returned to her desk. She hated the online database, and she really wished that the guy whose appendix had ruptured would come back and take over his job again. He was clearly much more competent at it than she was.

Pamela Morgan approached her, drumming her fingers against the desk. 'Ms. Selman, may I give you a word of advice?'

Antonia blinked in surprise. 'Sure.'

Pamela leaned forward and spoke quietly. 'You should be careful around Ms. Tovo. She's an excellent administrator, but she can get a little ... possessive about things, if you know what I mean.'

Antonia blinked. 'Do you mean the Mesoamerican exhibit?' *Because if that's the case,* she thought to herself, *Ms. Tovo should be the one curating it, not using me as a puppet.*

Pamela shook her head. 'Not exactly. Just ... be aware. That's all.'

The co-ordinator walked away briskly, as though the thirty-second meeting had never taken place. Antonia sat for a moment or two, wondering what her manager had meant by the cryptic message. Shaking her head, she pushed herself up from the chair and left for the Mesoamerican exhibit. Maybe doing some work with her hands would clear her mind.

ooooo

Traffic in the museum was slow during the winter seasons, and with the upcoming gala and the flurry of activity behind the scenes, many of the exhibits were closed to the public. So as Antonia walked the corridors towards the Mesoamerican exhibit, all was quiet, which she was grateful for. She had so much going on in her mind, the peace was welcoming.

As she moved between the rooms, she noticed there were several new additions to the collections. One wall displayed a large landscape of a battle scene. The painting was vivid and distressing. Men fighting in hand-to-hand combat with axe and bayonet; bloody and realistic. There was also a portrait of a young woman in tears. Her sorrow was so unmistakable that Antonia felt it reach out to her.

An old straw statue near the entrance to the foyer stood before her. Its face normally should have been impassive, a reminder of how some spirits were bigger than all of our problems and fears. But something about it was off today. The statue was *frowning*.

That can't be, Antonia thought. *It's just the angle I'm looking at it. If I move to the side...*

A sudden noise caused her to spin on her heel. It sounded distinctly like sniggering. Antonia scanned the length of the room, but the hall was as empty as before.

She turned back to the straw statue; but now it was smiling.

I will not be afraid like a little girl with a monster in the closet, she said to herself sternly.

Antonia picked up her pace, determined to get to her destination and ignore the insane sense of being observed. *There is no one here, there is no one here, there is no one..*

She burst into the Mesoamerican exhibit and ran directly into something large and alive. She yelped in terror, jumping back to see the thing she'd run into was a man. It was Hunter.

It was clear she'd startled him. He stepped back and his fist was raised above his face like he was trying to ward off an attack. *No,* Antonia thought, *he looks like he's ready to return the attack.*

'Ms. Selman? Are you alright?' Hunter asked, as he lowered his arm and brushed a hand distractedly over his suit coat.

Antonia's heart was beating wildly in her chest and her mouth had gone dry. 'Sorry. You surprised me.'

He raised his dark eyebrows, as though he was about to challenge who had startled whom, but instead he smiled and replied, 'My apologies. I wanted to check on some of my pieces.'

Antonia nodded, as though finding non-staff members in closed exhibits was completely natural. It wasn't of course, but she was too shaken up and embarrassed to make a scene about it. 'Which are yours?' she asked.

Hunter turned around to consider the room thoughtfully. 'Most of them, actually. But this one is my favorite.' He pointed towards a long copper mask. The eyes were slanted downwards, and the mouth was set in a straight line. Lines of gold inlay ran from the corner of the masks' eyes to the sides of the face, and more lines ran from the mouth to the chin.

'The Saber-Man Mask?'

'So, you know it?'

Antonia couldn't help but give him a look. 'He's a common myth throughout America's history, of course I know him.'

Hunter laughed unabashedly. 'My apologies, Ms. Selman. I don't often speak to people familiar with ancient American folklore.'

His good-natured embarrassment was contagious. Antonia relaxed. 'Well, he's not only ancient American,' she explained. 'Although he is interesting. He was a reminder to all warriors of what could happen if they allowed nature too much control over their spirits.'

'Don't listen to reason and you could become so blood thirsty you would kill your wife in her sleep, just like the Saber-Man.' Hunter said this in a low tone, almost like he was speaking more to himself than to her.

He looks sad, Antonia thought as she studied his face. Then she realized. *He looks like the man in my dream*, she gasped. *The one I left behind.*

Hunter glanced at her in question. She wrenched her attention back to the Saber-Man mask. 'The meaning of the legend is probably more along the lines of knowing that there are some things beyond our human reasoning.'

'Either way it's a cautionary tale,' Hunter said in the same low voice. 'Be careful when dealing with things outside of your control.'

He was so grave, so she tried to lighten the mood. 'My grandmother loved the Saber-Man. She was always telling me stories about creatures and spirits and how little girls like me should never try to engage with any of them.'

He looked away from her and back towards the mask. 'My ex-wife had a grandmother who sounds a lot like yours. A little strange, but great to have around.'

Antonia looked at him sideways. 'You're divorced?'

'Widowed,' he answered.

'I'm so sorry.'

'She died suddenly,' he said, turning to face her. 'If I'd been less... well, let's just say I wasn't around as much as I should have been.' He seemed apprehensive, even mortified that he'd shared that information with her.

As the day before, Antonia felt the same feeling wash over her like a tidal wave; heat, comfort, desire, and familiarity took over her body. Without thought, her hand reached up to press against his chest, and to her surprise she felt his fingers brush along her waist.

But as suddenly as the feeling appeared, it was gone. Antonia jerked back her hand. 'I... uh...'

'I should leave,' he said quickly. 'Have a good day, Ms. Selman.'

'Yes, you too...' she whispered to his retreating back.

He was half-way out the door when he paused and turned to face her. 'Ms. Selman. Are you going to the charity gala?'

'Yes. I'll be working, of course. Several of the staff will be attending.'

He nodded but didn't look her in the eye. 'Alright. Good. I'll see you there, then.'

'Yes,' Antonia answered again, but he'd already gone, and the room felt empty and cold without him there.

She sighed heavily. *What the hell was going on with her?* That was embarrassing and certainly not appropriate. *Maybe I should call in sick.* But the memory of Sonia's stern instructions put an end to that idea, and so Antonia threw herself into her work.

If there were any strange noises or unsettling feelings for the rest of the workday, she was too busy to notice them.

Chapter 6

'Welcome home, friend.' Katie slid out into the hallway in her socks with a look of triumph. 'You'll never guess what I got tod... Oh honey, wait. Are you okay?'

Antonia took off her coat. 'Yes, I'm fine..'

'Well you don't look fine. You look like your sleep schedule just got run over by a 16-wheeler van.'

'It's been an... interesting day.'

'Well then it's good timing, because I just got a $200 bonus from a client who's really impressed with my work, so we have something to celebrate as well as hearing about your interesting day.'

Antonio smiled, and ten minutes later they were in the living room clinking their wine glasses.

'So, what happened today?' Katie asked.

Antonia sighed heavily. 'I'm not even sure where to start.'

'Well the beginning is probably a good idea.'

'Okay... Well, for one thing I think my boss has control issues.'

'You mean the boss who is actually director of the company, but has this pet exhibit that she loves so much that she's completely unwilling to officially give it up and makes you, her assistant?'

'Okay yeah, you might have a point.'

Katie murmured affirmation. 'Do you think it's going to be a problem?'

'Well, I didn't...'

'Until...?'

'You know the guy I was talking about yesterday? The one who's a client?'

Katie's eyes widened. 'Yes. Go on.'

'I'm pretty sure my supervisor came by my desk to warn me about getting involved with things that my boss is already interested in and now I think she was talking about Hunter... I mean Mr Hunter.'

'I like just *Hunter*. That's so sexy. Anyway, do you think your boss has the hots for this Hunter? And she's noticed your interest in him... and the supervisor has noticed too and she's warning you off him?' Katie asked. 'Wow! Who knew the world of academia was such an intriguing lovefest?'

'I think that's taking it a bit far,' Antonia said with a laugh. 'Though I think it's about to get worse.'

'Worse for you or worse for your boss who's decided she wants to bang the handsome rich patron?'

Antonia rolled her eyes. 'I'm not sure. I ran into him today at the museum and...'

Katie lit up like a Christmas tree. 'Did you really?'

Antonia blushed. 'Nothing really happened, but...' The ghost of his fingers on her waist set her blood pumping. 'There's something there. I think he likes me.'

Her roommate squealed happily. 'Yes. Finally, a chance for you to use all those tips I've been giving you over the years.'

'He said he hopes to see me at the charity gala...'

If it were possible for Katie's eyes to get any bigger, they would have. 'Of course, the ball.'

'It's not a ball,' Antonia said disdainfully. 'It's a charity gala, which is entirely different.'

'I don't care what you call it,' Katie said. 'You're going to a ball with a fancy handsome man. We need to get ready, now.'

'Now?'

'Yes, now. Bring the wine.'

Antonia followed Katie into her room where she was already going through her clothing. For a girl who spent most of her days in front of a computer and dressed in sweats, she had an amazing wardrobe of glamorous gear.

'Now I think personally you should go kind of sexy. It's your first charity gala and you're fighting your boss for a man's affections...'

'It's also workplace function.' Antonia reminded her.

'But they expect you to dress the part, don't they?' Katie waved her off. 'Ball gown and all, right?'

'It isn't a ball,' Antonia repeated.

Katie mumbled, 'Alright fine, if we must. Now how are you going to do your hair?'

Antonio turned towards the mirror. Her thick dark hair was frazzled from all the stress and work at the end of the day, but she knew that with some care and attention, maybe pinned up at the side like so...

Suddenly she saw something. A flash of white that streaked from the mirror. She gasped and whirled around to follow it, but there was nothing there.

'Toni? Are you okay?' Her friend was looking at her in concern.

Antonio glanced around the room again and shrugged. 'Just tired, I guess.'

Her friend took her at her word and returned to the more pressing matter of preparing her roommate, friend, and love pupil for the fanciest night of her life.

Chapter 7

For the first time since she'd started to work at the museum, it finally felt the way it should. The area where the gala had been set was lit with gentle warm lights and guests in fine suits and beautiful dresses wandered about the rooms, pausing to admire a particular artwork or artifact. The pieces themselves responded with a mix of openness and coyness. Some painted women smiled at the viewers with bright eyes that invited more admiration. Other pieces smirked and glanced at the patrons with a side-eyed mischievousness. It was the kind of interaction Antonia was used to seeing in a museum, between patron and art. It was the reason she finally felt at home.

She wandered through the hallways, stopping to say hello to her fellow workers. A few of the older patrons were eager for an introduction. They wanted to meet the museum's newest curator, especially one so attractive.

Katie's one shouldered sheath of cream silk was elegant yet stunning in its simplicity. A cluster of diamantes on her shoulder, delicate diamond-drop earrings and a thin sparkling clasp that held back one side of her hair, was the only jewelry Antonia wore. The cream dress looked beautiful against her tanned skin and her bared shoulder was sensual without being overtly sexy. Katie had tried to talk her into a strapless red mini-dress, but Antonia firmly put her in her place. 'Remember, this is a work function.'

To make up for Katie's downturned face, Antonia had allowed her to do her hair. And she was happy she had. She always pulled her hair back in a ponytail or pinned it up at work because it got in the way, but tonight Katie had tamed it into a shining ribbon of satin that flowed down Antonia's back. She looked good and she knew it and she couldn't help but keep an eye out for a tall dark man who she hoped would like what he saw.

Antonia moved from room to room, answering questions about the exhibit and meeting guests. After nearly an hour she needed a break and discreetly lifted a glass of champagne from a passing waiter and made her way to the less crowded Mesoamerican display. Although these artifacts didn't attract the same numbers as the European art masters, to her they were far more interesting. They were among the oldest items on display and their history was one of ancient wisdoms and stories of eternal spirits. *We were here before you, and we will be here after you,* they seemed to say.

She was pleased with the way it had turned out, and she noticed with pride that the other visitors were enjoying themselves too.

'Ah, you're here.'

Antonia spun around to see Emmanuel Hunter standing behind her. He was wearing a well-cut suit, but the dress shirt didn't have a collar like everyone else. It made him stand out even more than usual. His presence was commanding, and she was drawn again to his dark eyes. They were mesmerizing and she fought to resist their pull.

'Enjoying the fruits of your labors?' he asked.

Antonia nodded. 'Ms. Tovo has a good eye.'

'Ms. Tovo has a good assistant,' he said. 'Tell me, how did you find this position?'

'Same as all of the other history majors; hard work, good recommendations and stupid amounts of good luck.'

Hunter chuckled. 'So, what was your field of study? Matriarchal cultures of the early Americas?'

'Close. Spirituality and religious practices of the early Americas.'

Hunter was skeptical. 'You don't seem the type.'

'Really? And what *type* is that?'

For a second, he looked embarrassed. 'What I mean is, you're not out in the field in overalls and sweat.' He recovered quickly and his gaze slid over her from top to toe, a faint grin lifting the corner of his mouth. 'Maybe I should have said that you don't *look* the part.'

Antonia smiled. 'Believe me, I've had my share of archeological digs and I will do many more. I love being out in the field and getting dirty.' She paused and he nodded for her to continue. 'My grandmother was the one who got me into it. She'd always tell me these ghost stories and fairy tales like they were a part of our family history.'

Emmanuel was intrigued. 'Were they?'

Antonia didn't feel like getting into her family's sordid past. 'Maybe. Probably. We've been here a long time. There's bound to be a black sheep or two in there.'

'So, you don't believe in ghost stories?'

Antonia thought back to the past few days, the recurring nightmares, the bizarre experiences in the museums and the white flash in her mirror. 'I believe in them as much as I should.'

Hunter studied her face. 'That's not answering the question.'

'It's a hard question to answer. You might as well ask me my views on God.'

He nodded in acknowledgement and changed the subject. 'So, the legend of the Saber-Man. How does that play into ancient religion?'

Antonia looked over at the mask on display. 'Probably not that much. He seems more like a boogieman than an actual religious figure. But he's a cautionary tale in a warrior culture. To beware of the 'id', as Freud would say.'

'Do you think these kinds of figures are man's attempt at making sense of the baser nature inside of him?'

The questions were like a burst of energy for Antonia. It was like being in school again, only better. 'It's possible. We all need some kind of signposts to guide us in the right direction. Killing your wife in cold blood is a pretty good incentive to not fall prey to the animal inside, no matter how great a warrior you are.'

'Do you think we can control that animal nature, Ms. Selman?' he asked in a low voice.

Antonia felt a shot of electricity shoot down her back. When did he come to stand so close to her? 'I think we try, but not everyone is perfect, Mr. Hunter.'

He chuckled and stepped back. She could breathe again. He was about to continue the conversation when Sonia swept into the room.

'Emmanuel, there you are,' she said, her eyes flitting back and forth between him and her new employee. 'Ms Selman. I didn't know you were here.'

Antonia looked at her boss and glanced down at the glass in her hand. 'I wanted to see how our exhibit was doing.'

'You mean my exhibit,' Sonia corrected her without a hint of malice in her face. She moved to Hunter's side and linked her arm through his. 'Hunter, I have someone I need to introduce to you. Shall we?'

Hunter nodded his acceptance and excused himself. 'We'll continue this later, I hope,' he said to Antonia.

As they left the room, Sonia looked back over her shoulder and said, 'Off you go, back to work. This isn't a social occasion for you.'

She was trying to work out whether she'd been insulted, and to what degree. She'd done all the work on this exhibit, not Sonia. But she was the boss. Did it even matter? She knocked back her drink and decided she needed some air.

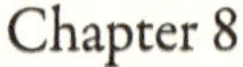

Chapter 8

In its past life, the museum had been a grand manor, built with oil money and sold to pay off failed speculation debts, generations in the making. The benefit of it formally being a beautiful home, was that it featured a magnificent garden as well. Antonia found her way to a quiet corner with high hedges, away from the lights and the noise of the people inside. She hugged her arms close to conserve heat in the mild winter night.

'Ma'am, are you... ? Oh, it's you.'

Antonia turned to see Miles, the same young security guard from her first day at the museum. He dropped the formalities and approached her. 'Are you lost again?'

'No.' She frowned. 'Are you going to try and kick me out?'

He could see she wasn't in the best of moods and nodded towards the party. 'Rough night?'

Antonia sighed.

'You shouldn't let them get to you. These rich schmoozy types can be hard to deal with and the academics are even worse. Either way they think they know everything.' He smirked. 'Present company excluded, of course.'

'Thanks. So, what are you doing here?'

'Right now, or in general?'

'General.'

'I'm using this job to help pay for school.'

'What are you studying?'

'English.'

Antonia grinned.

'What? Literature isn't more interesting than history?' he said in defense.

'Well...' Antonia rolled her eyes and lifted her hands to the sky. She tried to smile too, but doing so made the sound of her chattering teeth louder.

'Oh jeez, you're cold, aren't you?'

'No, I'm fine.'

'Here, take my coat.'

'No, really.'

Suddenly there was a sharp cracking sound behind one of the hedges. Miles and Antonia turned to see if one of the party guests had come to join them, but what they saw was nothing like the well-dressed gala guests.

Pushing the bush aside a slender woman appeared in front of them. Her head and shoulders slumped over like it was an effort to move at all. Her clothing was tattered and torn in odd places, and even though Antonia could have sworn the woman's dress was dirty, it shone bright and white.

'Ma'am, are you alr...' Miles began.

The woman snarled at him, her teeth broken and stained.

Antonia exchanged a look with Miles. Fear wrapped itself around her ankles like a cold snake slowly working its way up to her heart and lungs. 'Miles ...'

The woman in white turned to face them, her long brown hair covering most of her face.

The woman triggered something in Antonia's memory, an old story her grandmother had told her long ago. *Oh God. The White Lady.'*

Miles was afraid, but persistent. 'Ma'am, this is a closed event.'

The woman appeared to float over the hedge landing in front of them with a hard thump in front of them. She took a swipe at Miles and for a moment Antonia could swear she had claws.

Miles fell back against the hedge unconscious, his blue shirt growing darker and darker as blood poured from the wound the woman had inflicted. Antonia wanted to scream, but she felt like she was trapped in one of her nightmares, and all she could do was run. She turned and fled back to the house, but her high heels kept sinking into the cold ground. The White Lady wasn't far behind, snarling and muttering in an ancient gravely dialect. She wasn't speaking any language Antonia had heard before, but the meaning was clear; Antonia would be dead if she didn't run faster.

Awkwardly she kicked off her shoes and started to sprint, but the woman matched her pace. She kept trying to reach the party, but it only got farther away, just like a dream.

What do I do? What do I do? What do I do?

There was an abrupt change in the atmosphere, and what was cold was now burning hot. Antonia turned in time to see a man intercept the White Lady. He plunged the knife he held into the woman's breast at the same time she dug her claws into his shoulder, impaling him on her outstretched hand. There was a breath of time when it seemed that the man would fall, but it was the White Lady who shrieked in pain and disappeared before her eyes.

The man dropped to his knees, his shoulder spilling blood on the ground. 'Damn.'

Antonia's surroundings slowly returned. The lights of the party grew brighter, the cold sharper, and the sound of two people breathing hard in the winter air grew louder. 'Hunter,' she cried.

He turned to her, his black eyes ablaze in fury. 'Are you hurt?'

She stared at his shoulder. The wound beneath his ripped shirt was healing before her eyes. 'How?'

'Antonia! I need you to focus. Are you hurt?'

Realization hit her like a cold shower as she slumped against him, shock setting in. 'Oh my God. Miles.'

Hunter gripped her arms to keep her erect. 'What happened?'

'Miles, the security guard, he's hurt.' She pointed in the direction she'd come, only to realize she hadn't gone that far at all. *What did that woman do to me?*

Hunter was kneeling by Miles, who was as pale as dead grass in the moonlight. 'He needs a doctor,' Hunter said, pushing back his dark black hair as he dialed a number on his cell phone.

Antonia looked at the young man on the ground, his abdomen dark with blood. 'I think I'm going to be sick.'

'Not until you and I have talked,' Hunter shot back. He grabbed her roughly by the arm and pulled her away. 'Come on, we're going.'

'But what about Miles?'

The sirens of the ambulance screamed close by. 'He'll be OK now,' he muttered. 'Come on.'

'No,' Antonia pulled from his grasp. 'I am not going anywhere until I know he's alright.'

Hunter looked at her in frustration. 'And what do you want to say when the authorities ask you what happened?'

'The truth.'

He laughed at her. 'You're kidding.'

'No.'

'You're going to explain to the police that you were attacked by the ancient spirit of jealousy and rage, who proceeded to stab this young man and leave both you and I unscathed?'

Several responses shot through her mind, but none of them were satisfying and almost all of them were questions. The ambulance was getting closer, and she could hear the rising murmur of party guests wondering what the hell was going on outside. Antonia looked at Hunter and again she felt the indescribable tug pulling her towards him. This time she listened to it.

'Let's go.'

They hurried to his car, a sleek black beast in the winter star light. Antonia had barely shut the passenger door when Hunter ignited the engine and sped from the area through a side gate.

'Where do you live?' he growled. She hesitated. He was like a cougar. Controlled, but at this moment none of the urbane billionaire was evident. He frightened her a little, but excited her at the same time. 'Where do you live?' he asked with more insistence. She gave him the address and they drove in silence through the night.

Chapter 9

Antonia knew she'd done the wrong thing. It was weighing in her gut like a stone. She should have stayed with Miles, should have told the authorities what had happened, or at least an abbreviated version of it.

She glanced across at Hunter. His wound was completely healed, and there wasn't even a mark. *How on earth?*

'So, are you going to tell me why you were attacked?' The question was abrupt and his voice harsh.

Antonia winced. 'Excuse me?'

'I'm asking what you did that would motivate an ancient spirit to attack you.'

Antonia blinked stupidly. 'Nothing.'

'I don't believe it.'

'I'm not lying. And what do you mean spirit. It was just some deranged old woman who...'

'Who disappeared into thin air in front of you.'

Antonia stopped talking and crossed her arms.

'You have a degree in ancient spirituality, your family probably has a history of witchcraft, and your energy practically screams 'I have dabbled in things beyond my control", Hunter said sharply.

It took Antonia a moment to understand what he was implying. 'You think this was *my* fault?'

'Well, isn't it?'

'No, it is not,' she answered, her fury building.

Hunter was still skeptical. 'No ancient love rituals with your girlfriends in college? No bartering with a spirit to gain any favors?'

Antonia had never been more insulted in her life. If he hadn't been driving, she would have slapped him in the face. 'I do not *dabble*. If anything, my degree, which you hold against me, makes me the most qualified person in the world to know how much I should not *dabble*.' She spat out the last word like a dagger.

'I don't believe you.'

'You were clawed in the shoulder and there's not a mark on you. Explain that if you can. Maybe it's you who has done a deal with the devil.'

Hunter pulled hard on the steering wheel and skidded to a halt on the side of the road. He turned to glare at her in anger and for a brief moment she was afraid he was going to attack her.

Finally, he broke eye contact and stared straight ahead in silence. After the longest minute of Antonia's life, he slammed his fist on the car wheel and swore under his breath. After that, all the fight seemed to go out of him.

'I believe you.'

Antonia relaxed a little. 'Thank you.'

They sat together without speaking. Hunter seemed lost in thought; but she was very aware of him.

'So, are you going to explain any of this to me?' she asked.

'I'm not sure I can. There's a lot I don't know myself, but I can try. Where do you want me to start?'

'What happened to your wound?'

He paused and looked down, like he was just remembering he'd been stabbed. 'Oh, this? I'm immortal,' he answered matter-of-factly.

'A..ha,' she pressed herself against the car door, feeling for the handle. *He's crazy.*

'I was cursed. To live forever ... without her ... knowing what I'd done.'

A madman. Antonia hesitated, but only for a moment. If he was mad, then after tonight and what she'd seen, she was too. 'Who cursed you?'

He sighed and rested his head back against the leather. 'Hotah. He was my friend, or so I thought. He loved my wife, though I didn't know it at the time. His father was our tribal witchdoctor – a powerful healer, but also a weaver of the dark arts ... and he had learned from him.'

'Go on.'

Hunter turned to her. 'I'm telling you a fairy tale and you haven't batted an eyelid.'

'I've seen things throughout my life that I've ignored. Probably out of fear because I knew too much. My family history is as you have guessed; steeped in magic and mysticism. I kept away from 'dabbling' as you say, for my grandmother's sake, but I couldn't help being interested. That's why I chose the career path I did. I'm an academic, but I *know* there's more to this world than most of us realize.'

A look of relief washed over his features. 'Do you know how long it's been since I've spoken of these things? To anyone?'

She raised her eyebrow in question.

'It's been a very, *very* long time. There are whole centuries that are hazy for me, especially the ones immediately following my curse.'

Antonia was at a loss for words. 'Centuries?'

He shrugged it off. 'It's a blessing sometimes. No one wants to remember why he's called the Saber-Man.'

She gasped, 'You?'

'That's what they called me as they ran in fear. Back then, my... presence was a lot more intimidating.'

She didn't want to tell him that not much had changed. 'But you told me about your wife. Was she...?'

'Killed. Yes.'

'By...?' She stopped herself, but the rest of the statement was obvious.

'I don't know,' he answered. 'I've tried, but I cannot remember whether I was the one who murdered my wife.'

A bleak picture of Hunter's life began to form in Antonia's mind. Alone for centuries, unsure who had killed his wife. She wanted to comfort him but didn't know how. She reached out her hand and put it on top of his. He laced his fingers through hers as they sat in silence.

Eventually he spoke again. 'It was after a battle. I had led our people to a victory against raiders from another tribe, but I was injured in the process. I was brought back to our camp to have my wounds tended, but the fever took me. One night, against the healer's orders, my wife Cholena crept into the medicine man's tent to see me. I don't know what happened, but I was told that in my delirium I thought she was an enemy and I stabbed her with an arrow. In the morning my fever had broken, and I found her body beside me with an arrow from my quiver through her heart.'

He pressed his lips together in a hard white line and sucked in a painful breath before continuing.

'The healer's son – my childhood friend – accused me of her murder and convinced the tribe to banish me. It was he who put the curse on me – to live forever without her. Although the greatest curse was not knowing if I did what he said. I wandered alone, my legend growing as the years went on – and hence, the Sabre-Man was born.'

Antonia asked, 'The woman who attacked me. That was it the White Lady, wasn't it? My grandmother spoke of her.'

'Maybe. It was definitely an ancient vengeful spirit,' he replied. 'They creep up every once in a while, looking slightly different every time. Spirits change their appearances based on the culture. A few things remain unchanged though, and that's how you know what they are.'

'And you can see them?'

'It comes with the territory of being cursed. But what I don't understand is why it showed itself to you … and to Miles. I can only guess that your intense spiritual energy drew it to you.'

'What do you mean by that? What is my spiritual energy?'

'Everyone has a kind of energy that they put off. It's the part of them that engages with the world unseen, whether they know it or not. Yours is… particularly strong. It feels like the sun: brighter, older, and more powerful than anything around it. I felt it the moment I saw you. Even before I saw you. The office space was buzzing with it.'

Antonia frowned. She didn't feel that way. Yet the more she thought about it, the more it made sense. She'd always felt... different. Maybe this was why.

The light of the dashboard clock caught her eye. It was almost midnight. 'I should be getting home,' she said.

Hunter accepted it without question. 'Of course.'

They didn't speak to each other again until he pulled up outside her condo. He insisted on giving her his phone number before she left, and she didn't object. It was comforting to know that someone else would be able to shoulder this madness with her.

Antonia moved to get out of the car, but something stopped her. 'What was your name? Your real name?'

He debated with himself for a moment before answering. 'Nahuel.'

She nodded. 'Good night, Naheul.'

'Good night, Antonia.'

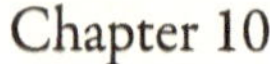

Chapter 10

Antonia visited the hospital the next day to see Miles. He was lying in bed watching some silly soap opera, when she knocked on his door.

'May I come in?'

He straightened up. 'Hey, what are you doing here?'

'I thought I would come see how you were doing,' she answered. 'I brought some flowers for you...'

'Thanks,' he said.

Antonia walked over to the nearby windowsill and placed her meager offering next to the other shinier gift store bouquets.

'Where did you get those?' he asked her.

'From our apartment garden.'

'They're still alive this time of year?'

She caressed the pale petals on one of the smaller ones. 'They hang on, yeah. How are you feeling?'

Miles winced and absent-mindedly scratched his chest. 'I'm alright. They stitched me up and put a big ol' band-aid on it. Did they, uh... did they find out what did it?'

Antonia shook her head. She had asked, but the nurses hadn't heard anything from the police. She wondered if she should tell him what Nahu- Hunter had told her, but she'd made an important decision that morning after remembering the words of her grandmother: *Don't get involved with the spirit world.*

It hadn't been an easy decision. There was so much going on, but she felt that fighting against the spirit world was a lost cause and she would follow the wisdom she'd followed her entire life.

She wouldn't even talk to Hunter again, she'd told herself. But she also hadn't deleted his number from her phone.

Miles sighed heavily and sank back into his bed. 'Well, I'm glad you're alright. The police said they couldn't find you.'

'They came to my house this morning,' she said. She didn't tell him what the conversation had been: *Who was the woman? Were you hurt? Why weren't you hurt? Why did you run away?* It had been an incredibly uncomfortable conversation, and Katie's questioning looks from the kitchen didn't help.

Antonia took a seat and looked down at her hands. 'Miles, I'm so sorry for leaving you like that—'

He waved her off. 'Don't be. She was after you too and you got help to me. I could have been lying there for hours.'

'I'm still sorry.'

'Well, you could make up for it by going to dinner with me,' he said. 'We could swap theories and things, maybe grab a nice drink.'

Antonia opened her mouth, closed it, and looked back down at her hands. 'I—I don't think that's a good idea right now.'

'OK sure, no problem. Maybe later.'

'I'll think about it though.'

But when she left his room ten minutes later, she knew she'd been lying. Miles was nice, and just earnest enough to be endearing. But he was so young, and she was so—

Ancient.

She shook her head. That was what Nahue- *Hunter*, had said to her. But she didn't really believe in all this stuff, did she? Spirituality was her field of study, not her way of life.

Then why am I trying so hard to avoid it?

She shook her head again. She'd deal with this later. For now, she wanted to go home and rest.

ooooo

The atmosphere in the office the next morning was grim. All their hard work had been tarnished by the strange attack. To make things worse, everyone appeared to avoid Antonia.

Although the police told her the details of the investigation would be private, she still felt the eyes of her co-workers on her. The sensation made her jumpy, and she called more attention to herself by spilling her coffee over her desk when Sonia Tovo called her.

'Ms Selman, my office. Now.'

Cursing under her breath, Antonia quickly mopped up the liquid before approaching the director's office.

'Close the door,' Ms. Tovo said firmly. She put her elbows on the desk and glared at her new assistant. 'I should fire you right now,' she stated.

'Wha-?'

'Your involvement in the incident on Saturday night is not a secret, Ms Selman,' her boss said. 'That kind of attention on our museum makes our patrons question the safety of their contributions to our establishment.'

Antonia's face burned, and she looked down at her hands. 'I'm so sorry—'

'Sorry doesn't cut it, Ms Selman,' the older woman snapped. 'And after all of that, you run off with one of our patrons.'

The heat moved from Antonia's face to her belly. 'I did not *run off* with anyone.'

Sonia raised a perfect eyebrow. 'You and Mr Hunter seemed to be on good terms earlier in the evening, and after the ambulance arrived, neither of you could be found.'

'Ms Tovo,' Antonia stated. 'I have done nothing but my best since I came here. I am sorry about what happened on Saturday, but that was not my fault. If you want to fire me, fire me based on my performance, not because of some assumption about my- my *intentions*.'

The older woman sneered. 'This is not some movie, my dear. You are not the young upstart who gets to come into my museum and win over everyone based on a half-baked dissertation and your young body.'

Antonia gripped the edge of her seat. 'You're right. I am young but I got this job on my results and reputation, not my body. If you fire me, I will still find a job. This is all about Hunter, isn't it? This has nothing to do with my work or even what happened on Saturday night. You think there's something going on between Hunter and me and you're jealous.'

Antonia stood up abruptly.

'Where are you going?' Ms. Tovo shouted.

'I'm taking the rest of the day off,' she shot back, and slammed the door behind her.

Chapter 11

Antonia barely made it to her car before bursting into tears. This was all too much. She was a good worker, a hard worker. Then why, *why* was this happening to her?

She needed to get some air. There was a park nearby she passed every day on the way to work. She'd planned to go there later in the year when the weather was warmer, but now seemed as good a time as any.

The park was a little sad in its winter cloak. The grass was yellow, and the trees were bare. She parked next to the nearest pathway, replaced her heels with flats and started walking.

The path led her through thickets and dead trees. Bird songs and rustling leaves were the only other sounds besides her sniffling. She was the only one around for miles. In other circumstances she might have enjoyed the peace, but today she was too distracted.

She kept thinking about what she'd said to Ms. Tovo. Why had she done that? She was torn between the idea that the woman deserved it and the knowledge that she'd been inexcusably *rude* to... her boss! She groaned, 'What have I done?'

This isn't me. She kept thinking. *I'm not like this. I'm a nice person, damn it.*

Eventually she looked around and realized the path had taken her to the edge of a small man-made lake. The grey winter skies were reflected in the water, robbing everything else of color. The continual flow and ebb was relaxing, so she stopped to watch. Then she saw it. Something white and floating beneath the water was moving toward her. In seconds it broke the surface and rose like the wraith it was. The White Lady.

Once her head appeared the rest was quick to follow, and Antonia watched in horror as she walked slowly across the water. The hatred and malice in the spirit's eyes transfixed her, and again she realized she couldn't move. She tried to scream, but it came out as a whimper. Antonia stared ahead, frozen in horror as the spirit continued on, coming closer with each step.

Suddenly a tiny white glow darted in front of her and raced towards the vengeful spirit. It was like the flash she'd seen in her mirror that day. Antonia forced herself to watch as the glow became a small boy who hurtled himself at the demon.

Before Antonia could yell at him to stop, he threw himself shoulder first into the woman. They crashed into the water, thrashing and wrestling each other deeper into the lake.

Antonia wrenched herself free from whatever power held her and ran into the lake after the boy. By now they were too far away, and with a final push the boy dragged the woman under with him, the water churning and bubbling, but soon all was quiet.

Antonia stood waist-deep in the lake, panting heavily. Where was he? Where was the boy who had saved her?

For a few agonizing moments everything was still, but suddenly he sprang from the water like a dolphin leaping into the air. Antonia cried out in relief, except now the boy was running towards her and he wasn't slowing down.

The last thing she remembered seeing were his black eyes as he barreled into her. When she came to, it was dusk and she was sitting on the ground against her car door, soaking wet and freezing. She scrambled to her feet, threw her car door open and searched frantically for her cell phone. He picked up on the first ring.

'Antonia?'

'Hunter,' she said through her terrified sobs. 'Hunter, I need your help.'

■———➤

Chapter 12

Emmanual Hunter's home was an altar to open space. It sat on the summit of a hill and every room had a view of the surrounding countryside. The rooms were warm and inviting and covering his walls were bold weavings and artifacts from around the world. It was the decoration of a man trying to connect to the past.

When Antonia arrived, Hunter was waiting for her and ushered her inside. His jeans and black T-shirt were a far cry from the suits he usually wore, but he was still imposing.

'What happened?' he began at once. 'Why didn't you let me come for you?'

Antonia touched his arm. 'I'm OK now.'

'God, you're freezing. Get out of those clothes now and into a hot shower.'

He pulled her to a bathroom hidden discreetly behind the wooden panels of the room. As he pushed her through the door he said, 'There's a robe on the back of the door. I'll get you a coffee and heat up some soup.'

'But...'

'No buts. We'll have time to talk later.'

Trying to break the tension in the face of his obvious worry, she said, 'Your home is beautiful.'

Hunter waved it off. 'I hope so; I've been working on it for centuries. Please, get warm. Then we'll talk.'

ooooo

Twenty minutes later, Antonia dressed in an oversized white bathrobe, was perched on a stool sipping hot soup. She'd used the bathroom hairdryer to get rid of most of the moisture from her hair but left it now to dry in soft waves around her face. She watched him silently as he moved about the large kitchen, preparing coffee and a plate of food for her to eat.

'You know your way around a kitchen,' she remarked.

'I've had years of practice.'

He placed two coffee mugs and plate on a tray and walked to a small sitting room overlooking the valley below. 'Come on.' He nodded for her to follow. 'We may as well be comfortable before you tell me what happened. I have a feeling I'm not going to like what I hear.'

Antonia sunk into the plush sofa curling her feet under her. She sipped her coffee before speaking. 'That day at the gala. I had a feeling you wanted to leave me to my fate.'

There was no bitterness in her voice or her thoughts. How many spiritualists and white witches had she met over the course of her research? How many of them had she left to their own devices?

I didn't take it seriously then, she thought.

'Yes,' he admitted, as he took a seat next to her on the sofa. 'It was wrong of me. I was... afraid.'

The admission made Antonia smile. 'Me too.'

Hunter leaned back, his outstretched hand resting on the couch above her shoulder. The proximity gave her comfort, and she began to relax more. 'Tell me what happened,' he said.

She explained to him about the return of the White Lady, and how the little boy had saved her. When she finished, he sighed deeply and ran his hands through his dark hair.

'You're sure it was a boy you saw? Not just the light playing tricks?'

'No, it was definitely a child,' she said. 'What do you think he was? I know he wasn't human.'

Hunter shook his head. 'No, it wasn't. My best guess is that it's a protective spirit, but I can't be sure.'

Antonia had studied protective spirits before. They were usually characterized as 'good', which was a comforting thought. Others, however, were just ambivalent, choosing to protect people as long as they felt like it.

'What should I do?' she asked.

The look on his face told her that she wasn't going to like what he was about to say. 'I think we should summon this vengeful spirit and figure out why it's attacking you.'

Antonia's heart stopped. 'You want to—No!'

'We can do it safely,' he continued. 'I have the necessary materials, and we can bind it as soon as it appears.' His hand kneaded the back of her neck. 'Antonia, they're going to come for you anyway.'

His hand felt warm, and the movement of his thumb against skin set her nerves on fire. He stared at her, searching her face like a man looking through a keepsake box for an old memory. 'Why are you helping me now?' she asked.

He smiled. 'To make up for some of my own past sins, perhaps. And because I know what it's like to be cursed and not really know why.'

He began kneading her neck again and the motion triggered a feeling of safety. 'Fine,' she said quietly. 'Let's get this over with.'

ooooo

The problem with this plan as far as Antonia could tell, was that she was only alright with it when Hunter was literally leading her by the hand. But at some point, he had to let go, and now she was sitting on the recliner in his office, watching as he pushed all the furniture to the side to clear a space for the summoning ritual.

'What happens now?' she asked.

'We call,' he replied. 'It answers, we capture it, and we question it. And if that doesn't work, I have this.' He pulled up his shirt to show her the bone dagger he had used to dispatch the White Lady before. It was tucked into the waist of his jeans.

He'd told her it was made of blessed animal bone and was very powerful, but all she was thinking was how the muscles of his abdomen moved under his tanned skin. As her pulse quickened, she mentally argued with herself. *This isn't the time to start lusting after him.* To cover her discomfort, she blurted, 'How long will this take?'

He chuckled darkly. 'Tired of me already?'

'No,' she answered quickly, which amused him a little. 'I just want to be done with *this*.'

'I hate to tell you,' he answered, 'but I'm not sure you're ever going to be done with 'this'. Once spirits show themselves to you, they tend to do it over and over again, until their reason for stalking you is completed.'

As Hunter answered her questions, he dipped his hands into an old clay jar he'd taken from the vault in his office. He then walked slowly around the hardwood floor, sprinkling the dust in the shape of a circle.

'What is that?' Antonia asked.

He stood up and dusted off his hands. 'Very, very old dirt.'

She watched him in silence as he finished the circle, drawing an extra circle around the dust with an inky black liquid, also from his vault. Her heart was in her throat. She couldn't shake the idea of her blood staining the nice carpet beneath Hunter's desk.

'Here.' He brushed aside her dark hair and made a small mark on her pulse points with the liquid. It smelled like lavender. 'For extra protection,' he said.

Antonia was too worried to speak, so she just nodded.

'Are you ready?' he asked, taking her hands, and putting more liquid on her wrists.

'I guess.'

He gripped her hands softly. 'Don't worry. We'll be alright.'

Hunter stepped back and indicated the circle. 'Once this begins, I'll be the one asking the questions. Stay behind me, don't look directly at it, and don't be afraid.'

She gave a hollow laugh. 'I'll do my best.'

He grinned and then placed a bowl of water in the center of the circle. 'Lake water,' he explained. 'Let's not make this any harder for her than we have to.'

He pulled the t-shirt over his head and threw it aside. His body was hard and muscular, and the bone knife glowed against his dusky skin. Closing his eyes, he stretched out his arms towards the circle of dust and began to speak quietly to himself in a language Antonia had never heard.

The effect was almost immediate. The temperature of the room dropped dramatically, and frost began to form on the windows. *She must really want to be here,* she thought.

Hunter kept speaking and didn't stop when the head of the White Lady appeared in the bowl of water. Antonia looked away but it was hard not to feel the presence of the spirit. She was a magnet, a negative charge to Antonia's positive one.

A startled shriek made Antonia jump. The White Lady must have realized she was trapped.

For his part Hunter didn't miss a beat. 'Spirit, if you want to be free then you must tell me what you know.'

The spirit wailing in agony, replied in gibberish.

'A bargain is a bargain,' Hunter continued. 'You will be released back to the waters you came from. Now tell me why you're hunting this woman?'

The White Lady moaned, her words coming out fast and hateful. As she spoke, the energy in the room seemed to change. It was still cold, but silent and heavy, like the air before a storm. Only the sound of the White Lady's voice was heard, like a siren in the distance getting deeper, louder and more animal-like.

Antonia couldn't take it anymore. She squinted at the spirit and gasped. It wasn't a woman anymore, but a huge formless thing without a face.

The spirit spoke, its voice rattling inside Antonia's bones. 'NAHUEL.'

Hunter was as rigid as stone, his face white with fear and rage. '*You,*' he hissed. 'What do you want?'

Although the spirit had no face, Antonia felt it's sickening grin. 'TO FULFILL THE CONTRACT, I MADE LONG AGO.'

A flash of light filled the room. Antonia was flung backwards and crashed into the glass cabinet behind her. She covered her head as glass rained down, slicing tiny nicks into her arms and hands. The laughter of the spirit grew loud in her head, but it was not enough to drown out the screams of Hunter.

He was doubled over on the floor, clutching his abdomen. The spiritual presence was overwhelming, and Hunter was in trouble. They were both in trouble if she didn't do something.

Gritting her teeth, Antonia pushed herself from the floor and tried to reach him. She felt like she was walking through thick molasses, her steps slow and heavy. As she reached Hunter's side, the White Lady appeared before her again, her fingers were claws as she raised her arm to strike. Antonia's hand gripped the handle of the bone knife and pulled it from the band of Hunter's jeans. She struck upward with all her strength, burying the blade deep into the body of the wraith. An unearthly scream signaled her success as the White Lady disappeared in a cloud of white mist.

The blade dropped from Antonia's hand as Hunter summoned the strength to lunge at the dark mist that now solidified into the shape of a Native American man in animal skins. His face and bare chest were painted with ochre and blood. His long dark hair was matted with mud and small bones were tied within the filthy strands. He carried no weapon, yet his sinister powers continued to wreak havoc on Hunter's body. His screams of pain were torture to her ears.

What could she do? She didn't know enough of the spirit world and the dark powers; the bone knife was gone, and she was helpless – unless ... Antonia's desperate gaze fell on the smashed cabinet and Hunter's most prized possession – the stone arrow of the Sabre-Man.

She moved quickly and reached to lift it from its resting place. As her hands held it, the pressure in the room suddenly released and a mighty howl came from the dark spirit, but she didn't have time to think about that.

In seconds she was hit by another wave of energy; a jolt of lightning that started in her heart and zipped to every nerve in her body. Memories started surfacing of prairies and wild rivers and sunsets more brilliant than anything she'd ever seen. Pictures moving so quickly she felt dizzy. A mother's hand braiding her hair, a grandmother mashing up corn and telling her stories of spirits. They were similar to her own memories, yet completely foreign. Then a man stood before her, a man with a noble bearing, a square jaw and a mischievous glint in his eye. Her man. He was the man from her dreams and the man who was dying on the floor in front of her.

She grasped the arrow and turned towards the spirit. Could she feel fear coming from the thing in front of her? Dread?

Yes, I can, she thought. *It's afraid. It's afraid of me!*

More new memories seamlessly slid into Antonia's consciousness and rage filled her body as she witnessed them. She raised the arrow and ran at the spirit, plunging the stone head deep into its heart. The thing screamed and with one final burst of light, disappeared as the arrow fell to the ground.

Antonia dropped to her knees and wrapped her arms around Hunter. Then frantically she pulled his face to hers, searching him quickly for injuries. 'Nahuel, are you alright? Are you hurt?'

He started back at her, and she watched as his expression turned from one of disbelief to joy. 'I was right, wasn't I? It is you.' He drew in a sharp breath. 'Cholena?'

'Yes, my love. I have come back to you.'

Epilogue

The arrow of the Sabre-Man, the arrow of Nahuel the warrior was once again behind glass in the den of Emmanuel Hunter's home.

Hunter held his champagne glass high and looked into the eyes of his wife Antonia. 'A toast, my love.'

'To what? We have so much to be grateful for.' Antonia snuggled within the circle of his strong arms.

'To our future together. To the future children who will carry on our memories and most of all, my eternal thanks to my beautiful wife for lifting the veil of guilt that has clouded me for so long.'

Antonia's eyes misted. 'Ah Nahuel, how cruel was that curse ... how bitter with hatred was Hotah, that he made you believe you had killed me, when it was *he* all along who had done the deed.'

'He loved you, Cholena. And if he couldn't have you for himself, then no-one could.'

'And whenever I tried to return to you over the centuries, he and his dark forces always managed to stop us from re-uniting.'

His lips gently touched hers. 'But not this time.'

She smiled against his mouth. 'And never again. The curse is broken, and we have the rest of our lives together.'

'The rest of our lives,' he answered as he pulled her against him and captured her lips again.

The End

Other books from Elli Buchanan:

Re-Runners

(Paranormal Time-Travel Series)

To View Re-Runners VIDEO BOOK TRAILER

Go to: http://www.booksbyellibuchanan.com/rerunners-video.html
To get your **FREE** copy of Re-Runners First Life, go to:
www.booksbyellibuchanan.com

If you had the chance to go back and relive the last 25 years of your life, retaining all the knowledge and memories you have now; would you make different life choices?

Three very different people from different locations die at the same moment in time and re-awaken at that moment, only it is 25 years earlier. Two men and one woman are reborn in their young and healthy bodies, but their minds retain the memories of their previous lifetime. Will the abused wife choose a different path? Will the stockbroker choose a different wife? Will the serial killer continue on his spree of murder?

Follow the journey of three Re-Runners; Kate, Dylan and Christian through this series of rediscovery, changing fates and finding each other.

Love Me, Love My Sister

(Romance Novella)

It's been 10 years since Beth Taylor has seen the man she secretly gave
her heart to as a teenager and now he's her boss.
Their relationship grew from the letters that passed between them when
he was fighting in Vietnam and she was a high school senior; but he
believed the letters were coming from Beth's beautiful older sister
Jennifer, whom he had met in a Sydney nightclub the night before he
was deployed.
Can Beth put her feelings behind her and work with Nic?
When Jennifer comes to town with Nic in her predatory sights, will Nic
forgive the woman he believes broke his heart and again fall under her
spell?
Can Beth stand by and watch it happen or should she tell him the truth
of the deception she and her sister committed all those years ago?

Forbidden Mortal

(Story 1 in the Sky Kingdom Short Story Series).

The enmity between the Eagle Convocation, the Hawk Cast and the Owl Parliament has governed the sky civilizations for hundreds of years. During their lifetime, the rulers of the Convocation and the Cast had formed an uneasy alliance. To join their offspring in marriage would unite the two powerful nations and give them the strength to defeat and enslave the mighty Owl Parliament ruled by the blood thirsty Caradas family.

Lady Hawk Salima Isolde fought against this union as did Egypt Volker, the son and now ruler of the Eagle Convocation. As children they played as companions, yet neither would be forced into a marriage not of their choosing. On the death of her father, Salima rules the Hawk Cast with a more benevolent hand, yet the threat of war is always on the horizon. The bird shapeshifters are a species born of bloodlust. The battle, the kill and the prey are part of what they are, yet Salima fought this side of herself. The bloodletting sickened her, and the ever-present threat of war and enslavement of her people was a constant distress.

She knew of the folklore. There was a way to end the existence of the shape-shifting creatures of the sky. No more fighting, no more fear of being enslaved by another shape-shifting avifauna order. All it would take is one human—just one, to stop Parliament, the nation of shape-shifting owls from enslaving the Convocation and the Cast, condemning them to be bondsmen for as long as time should endure and for Salima to be free of the confines of remaining a hawk-woman forever.

An unlikely and initially dangerous encounter with a human in the forest opens the door for Salima to put her plans into motion. However, what she does not bargain for is the effect that Rolfe Cedric, a mere human, will have on her sensibilities.

Can Salima follow through with her plan to use Rolfe to end the threat of the Cast's enslavement by the Owl Parliament and at the same time free herself from her own personal captivity, or will she spare the man who has evoked feelings in her she was unprepared for and unable to fight against?

For your copy of any of Elli's books

Go to:

http://www.booksbyellibuchanan.com/books.html

Hello from Elli...........

www.booksbyellibuchanan.com

Did you enjoy this story?

If so, I'd really, really appreciate it if you would tell your friends and let the world know, by taking the time to write a review on the site you purchased this book from. ☺

Reviews are important to self-published authors. It gets our name out there, spreads the word about our books and pushes the enthusiasm button to keep us writing, writing, writing.

Thanking you in advance.

To get in touch with Elli and find out when new books are launched go to:

www.booksbyellibuchanan.com and join her Readers Group.

Visit Elli's wider world. Chapter excerpts, silly quips, insights.

Drop in and 'like' my Facebook page:

https://www.facebook.com/booksbyellibuchanan

See all Elli's books on:

www.amazon.com/author/ellibuchanan

Cover Design by: Kirsten McClure

---

1. http://www.booksbyellibuchanan.com/

ABOUT THE AUTHOR

The ideas for several stories came about when my man and I were floating around on a boat in the Mediterranean for sixteen months. Plenty of time for the creative juices to flow and undoubtedly the experience of a lifetime, but before any of those ideas became fully fledged books; we returned to Australia and the real world of jobs and in my case, opening a small business.

Five years later, the beloved business has sold and now it's time to write again.

Love Me, Love My Sister was a beginning, until my 'evil twin' emerged and wanted to write something edgier with murder, mayhem and mystery and the Re-Runner Series was born. The pleasure I get from writing continues.

I hope you enjoy reading this collection of novellas and short stories, while I decide which genre, I best like writing.

Elli

www.booksbyellibuchanan.com

www.ingramcontent.com/pod-product-compliance
Lightning Source LLC
Chambersburg PA
CBHW021345160726
47994CB00007B/2851